Ann Obayuwana was born in Liverpool and lived there till she was 14 years old. She moved with her family to Skelmersdale and then later moved to London. After a lifetime of working in social housing, her last job was being the head of resident service at YMCALSW. She and her husband moved back to her birthplace. During lockdown, Ann thought back to her school days and how she used to love writing stories. So, she thought she would set herself a challenge and found she still enjoyed writing. Now she hopes others will enjoy it too.

To my husband, Isaac Obayuwana, who had always supported me and given me confidence to chase my dreams.

Ann Obayuwana

MIRROR OF HOPE

Hope deferred makes the
heart sick (Proverbs 13 v 12)

AUSTIN MACAULEY PUBLISHERS™

LONDON • CAMBRIDGE • NEW YORK • SHARJAH

A CIP catalogue record for this title is available from the British Library.

ISBN 9781398446120 (Paperback)
ISBN 9781398446137 (ePub e-book)

www.austinmacauley.com

First Published 2022
Austin Macauley Publishers Ltd®
1 Canada Square
Canary Wharf
London
E14 5AA

To Austin Macauley Publishers who took a chance on a
new author.

Marcos Whyte was looking for a mirror for his art studio. He had seen many new ones but he wanted something that had some age to it, he went to boot sales, charity shops, Jumble sales, but nothing felt right.

As he worked in his studio, which overlooked his rambling garden, he saw something glittering in the sun. He went to see what it was, maybe it was a reflection from the window or a pool of water. He walked down the wet winding path to the area he could see out of the window.

It had rained all night and the garden had that lovely after rain smell, the sun was shining and the water glistened on the leaves of the trees, the fruit trees were laden with fruit nearly ready to harvest. He finally got to the back of the garden and pushed away the ivy growing on the wall and there was a mirror. How it got there, however, was a mystery. Marcos was sure he had worked in the garden in that area, so how did this mirror get there? He picked up the mirror, it had some foxing and a small crack in a corner but it was just what he was looking for.

Marcos carried the mirror into his studio, he tried it on every wall and finally decided the right place was on the wall opposite where he painted. The mirror had such depth and reflective qualities, he decided he wouldn't have to keep searching for something that had appeared out of nowhere.

Marcos did oil paintings, he had a wide portfolio, he did commissions, he did portraits but he got the most joy out of doing fantasy paintings. He had finished his latest commission which was a landscape of Barbados from a photo. It was sitting on his easel so he went in to pack it up. As he was sitting facing the painting, he heard a noise from behind him, and could feel a warm breeze and the smell of the sea. He turned and saw his painting in the mirror, with the tide coming in and out, and the sun shining.

He went over to look into the mirror, and as he did, he was drawn into the mirror and the next minute he landed on a beach. He could feel the sand in his toes, he was lying on a towel with a bottle of water and shoes at his side, he didn't know how he got there and thought he must be dreaming but how can he feel sand in his toes and the sun on his face.

He got up and someone called his name.

"Marcos, do you want fresh coconut?" He looked around and a gorgeous young woman who knew his name, and that he loved fresh coconut.

She came running over and planted a kiss on his lips. He was surprised but he kissed her back. Suddenly, he knew her name was Lacy.

He pulled her down onto the towel, she laughed at him and grabbed the water bottle and poured it on his head. He was shocked. He was sitting on a beach in the landscape he had painted, exactly how he didn't have time to try and figure it out.

Lacy got up and grabbed him and told him they need to go as the nanny was dropping off the children at the house and they needed to get back.

He stood up and picked up the towel and followed Lacy to the car. She threw the keys to him, he asked her if she could drive, she was happy to do it and they drove home in silence.

Marcos was trying to get his bearings, he didn't recognise anywhere as they drove away from the beach. Lacy pulled into the driveway and before him was a large imposing house.

A car drew up behind them and two boys came running up to meet them, Marcos said hi and hoped someone would tell him their names.

The nanny shouted, "Glyn and Alan, you forgot your swimming gear". Marcos now knew their names but he had never seen this house before. How was he going to act like he knew where everything was? How was he not going to look stupid?

He followed Glyn and Alan into the house and he looked at his hand and noticed a wedding ring. This made him panic. How did he end up here? He walked into the house, it was open plan so no need to worry about the downstairs but how was he going to navigate his way around?

He went into the sitting area and sat on the corner of the leather couch, Glyn was shouting from upstairs for his dad. So Marcos followed the voice and Glyn was in one room and Alan in the next one.

Glyn told his dad that he wanted to do a lifesaving swimming course and wanted to do his bronze, silver and gold medals. Marcos was delighted and asked him why he had chosen to do this. Glyn said he wanted to be just like him, as he saw him save a lady from the sea.

Marcos couldn't even swim but this was a dream, so maybe here he was a better person, in reality he wasn't even married.

Alan called him and asked if he could go to work with him next week when he returned to the mayor's office. Marcos was taken aback how he ended up being a Mayor of Bridgetown. He said yes to Alan.

Lacy was shouting from downstairs that dinner was to be served. Marcos looked into the other rooms and found what he believed was his and Lacy bedroom.

He heard the children running down the stairs and he followed them. On the table was a wonderful dinner brought in by the chef,

"Wow!" Marcos said. It looked beautiful, he enjoyed eating with his family.

After dinner it was all cleared away and they all went to sit on the couch and Lacy put on a movie. Marcos could feel himself relaxing and looking forward to what adventures were in store. The evening went well and it was bedtime and they all retired to their rooms.

Marcos was overwhelmed to have such a wonderful life and family. Lacy came up while Marcos was in the bathroom, she undressed and climbed into bed. Marcos went downstairs to look in every area of the house as he didn't want to be caught out as a fraud. By the time he had checked everywhere, Lacy was fast asleep. Marcos put his head on the pillow thinking it was going to be wonderful life, good job, and beautiful family. He fell fast asleep.

He shook his head and he was in his front room sitting in his favourite armchair, looking around and couldn't believe where he was. He couldn't believe it was a dream. It was so vivid, he had a wife and children, and was happy in Barbados, and his real life was lonely and boring living in Lancashire on his own.

He got up and pinched himself, the doorbell rang and it was the customer coming for her painting of Barbados. He showed her the painting which she loved and was happy to take it home. It was a present for her husband. It was where they went on honeymoon and the picture brought back that romantic time.

After she left Marcos went to tidy his studio and strangely found some specks of sand on the floor by his easel, he couldn't figure out where the sand had come from. He thought maybe it was in the bag his customer brought the photo in.

Marcos had a lot of friends in the village where he lived, he loved his life but it was lonely. He thought about getting a cat, but he didn't think it would help, it was usually late at night he was lonely. Someone offered him a puppy, but he turned that down, his family had always had a dog but he didn't have the time to teach a puppy. Also he didn't think it would give him the love of a family which he didn't know he needed until he had that dream.

Marcos went out with his sketch book into the Ribble Valley and the Trough of Bowland. The area was known for its beautiful lanes, scenery and its forest. It was an area that seemed to be a big secret, he never understood why, and he took lots of photos and made some rough sketches.

He saw lots of walkers, some on their own, and others in groups, some with dogs, it gave him such peace. What a wonderful part of the world he lived in, he had given up on love.

He so wanted to meet his soul mate, someone just like Lacy, he told himself you can't live in a dream and get on with his life, but he couldn't get that desire removed from his heart.

Marcos got home before the rain set in, he stood at the window looking out on his wilderness garden. He wished he was a gardener, he loved messing around in the garden and thankfully his parents were gardeners and helped to keep the garden from falling into disarray. They lived in Lancaster which was about one hour away.

He longed to have a marriage like theirs. Wilfred and Doris met at a ramblers meeting. Wilfred helped her over a stile and they began to chat, it turned out they had a lot in common, Wilf said it was love at first sight but Doris says it wasn't for her, he seemed too nice and she had been hurt before and found it hard to trust.

She had met whom she thought was a nice man, who turned out to be a fraud and a swindler. She had met him at a church she had attended for years, he had said he was a lawyer and a preacher. He had recently moved into town. He was so charismatic and everyone loved him, so she was so flattered that he had chosen her, there were more beautiful women in the congregation. She didn't understand why he wanted to be with her., They went out, they went to the theatre, films, walks in the park. He took her sailing on Windermere Lake, he was always a gentleman, never crossed his boundaries. He knew she was a virgin and was waiting for the wedding night. He bought her flowers, her parents loved him and they hoped he would be their future son-in-law. It all seemed to be going well but there started to be whispers about him that he wasn't what he seemed, he had a past that he was running from, he heard the rumours and told her that it was only jealousy and she ignored the whispers but something in her put her on red alert.

He carried on being a gentleman, he never changed. One day he went to see Doris's parents to ask for her hand in marriage. They were delighted and gave him their blessing.

Doris came home from work, she was a school art teacher and she shouted to say she was home.

Her mum came out and said, "Julius was here and we have given him permission to propose to you."

Her mum was so happy but something in Doris's heart didn't feel right but she pushed that feeling away and went into the room. She saw her dad with a glass of whiskey in his hands and Julius was sitting in the armchair opposite him drinking whiskey.

He put it on the table next to the armchair and stood up and kissed her on the cheek. He then got down on one knee and held out a ring asking her to marry him. Even though inside she was screaming no, no but she felt pressured into saying yes. Her parents hugged her and him and checked out the ring, it was big and impressive.

Doris put a smile on her face and accepted the congratulations, and then there was talk on setting a date for the wedding. Doris really couldn't get over the uncertainty in her heart, maybe it was just nerves.

Julius wanted to get married quickly, he said he loved her so much and wanted to be with her for the rest of their lives. She spoke to her mum about her apprehension but she thought it was nerves and she would be okay once the wedding was over. She talked to her friend but she also reassured her that it's just wedding nerves.

So the plans started and rolled on, Doris's parents had saved enough for their only daughter's wedding. So Julius only had to get himself to the church on time. They were even going to move into her parents' house until Julius sold his home in London.

So off to the wedding shop to buy the dress. She tried at least seven on, until she found the one. Her mum cried when she found the one. Next the veil, shoes and off to do cake tasting.

Julius wasn't there for most of the preparation for the wedding. Doris's parents arranged the flowers, church, cars everything. Invitations were sent out and the day came around quickly. Julius came around on the eve of the wedding and brought a bottle of whiskey and a large bunch of flowers, Doris was still having her worries but pushed them to the back of her mind.

At ten thirty Julius left to go home, he kissed Doris on the cheek and said he would see her in the morning. The next morning Doris was up early. Her mum found her sitting on the bed, she said she wasn't going, her mum put it down to pre-marriage nerves, and she wiped her eyes and her friend came to do her makeup and her hair. The time went so fast and she was ready. Her mum went ahead and her dad was waiting at the bottom of the stairs. He looked up and saw a beautiful bride and he was so overwhelmed. He took her hand, opened the door, and led her down the path to the waiting horse-drawn carriage.

The neighbours were out on the street cheering her on. They arrived at the church and the doors were opened to a beautiful flower-filled church and Julius was waiting at the front of the church. He smiled as he saw her on the arm of her dad. She stood next to Julius and the minister started the service, he started the wedding ceremony and welcomed everyone and he started to ask if anyone had any reason why they couldn't get married.

Suddenly there was a mighty bang on the door and in marched a heavily pregnant women with two toddlers, screaming, "Stop the wedding! Julius is married to me!"

Doris knew that she should have never agreed to marry him, she should have listened to her heart. The minister stopped the wedding and took them all into his office to find out what was going on. It turned out Julius was married, he wasn't a lawyer, and he had studied Law for at least one year at university. He had spent time in a sect which drummed the bible into him and he had met Dawn there and they got married at a registrar office after a whirlwind romance and they lived in London in a council flat in Stonebridge.

He had been missing for six months. Dawn reported him missing and they had searched for him. No news until he used his bank card to hire a morning suit, the police saw the transaction and contacted the tailor who told them of the wedding, so they had contacted Dawn who arranged for a friend to drive her to the church hoping to get there on time.

Doris wasn't broken hearted, she was just sorry her parents had spent their savings and she couldn't get it back. They seemed more upset than her, they wanted to console her but it was them that needed consoling.

They went into the main church and told everyone that the wedding was off and invited them all to the church hall for a party.

The guests were confused, so the minister told them Julius was not who he had seemed and he was returning to London with his wife. Doris was surrounded by guests who wanted to offer her their condolences but she said she had been lucky and they should not be worried. She left the church with her parents to change and go back to the church hall for a party.

That is why Wilfred had to fight for Doris's affection, it took him three years to prove his love and finally she agreed to marry her.

He paid for everything, he said he was sure she was the one. He wanted to grow old with her and he had been saving for a house as he didn't think he would ever find the one. He had enough for a small wedding and a deposit on a house. She did love him but once bitten is twice shy. Eventually she agreed and they were married with her parent's blessing.

Marcos wanted a marriage like his parents but he didn't think it would ever happen, not like in his dream. Well life goes on and he is meeting a potential customer. He had an email requesting an appointment, they had seen his work online and had attended one of his exhibitions in Lancaster.

He set off to the customers' home, it was a couple who had been married six months and very much in love. They wanted an oil painting of the church. They were married at the Holy Trinity Church in Hoghton near Preston. They wanted to include the path to church door, and an oil painting of Hoghton Tower. Marcos was delighted to get the commission and asked them if they had photos, they gave him some of their wedding photos. He told them the time frame in which he would be able to complete the paintings.

The next day Marcos went off to sketch and photograph the church and the tower. It was a lovely drive and he missed the turning for the church even though they sat nav in the car told him to turn left, so he turned around at the entrance to Hoghton Tower, at least he wouldn't miss that place.

So he drove back to the church and parked in the car park. He took out his camera, sketch book and other equipment. The church entrance was past a very neat and tidy graveyard. He spent some time taking photos and sketches. It was a very warm day and Marcos began to feel hungry but he hadn't packed anything, so he wondered if there was somewhere to get a sandwich and a cup of tea. He didn't think he had seen any such place as he had driven up to the church. He wondered if Hoghton Towers had a café or it was just a wedding venue. So he drove over to the Tower and started the drive up to the Tower. It was a long, sweeping drive, it was like the driving up to a stately home in a Victorian novel.

He parked at the front of the Tower and saw signs of a café, so he packed his equipment and followed the signs. He was surprised at how beautiful it was, he didn't even know it was not far from Preston.

He entered the building, it had wood-panelled walls, large stone fireplaces and stone flags. It was going to be a pleasure to paint. He got himself a sandwich and a cup of tea and he spied a wonderful death by chocolate cake which he thought he might come back and get a slice to take home.

He spoke to one of the guides and he suggested areas around the tower where most couples have their photos taken, and directed him to some hidden places in the woods surrounding the tower. So off he went to find these places. He spent a lot of time wandering around the woods and the tower, where he took lots of photos and sketches. He sat down on a bench and drifted off and slept for a short while, but long enough to miss out on the death by chocolate. The café was shut when he walked past, so went on to the car and drove home to start the paintings. He still had other paintings to finish before he could start these ones.

Marcos was painting a fantasy oil, lots of colours, flowers, fairies, butterflies and a sleepy willow tree. It was for the exhibition he was planning. He needed to just finish it with a couple more flowers, and put in the shining sun. Having finished the painting he sat down on a chair and he felt the sun on his back and a warm breeze rustling through his hair but the room was cold and it was dark.

The next minute he was sitting with his feet in a stream and flying past him were butterflies and humming birds. He looked up to the sky, it was multi-coloured and there were rainbows all over the sky. He lay back onto the soft ground and closed his eyes, he heard a voice calling him Marcos.

He opened his eyes and there stood a fairy, beautiful with long yellow hair, wearing what looked like a daffodil. The most amazing thing was that as he looked into her eyes he knew that this was Lacy. How had she got into this dream?

She took him by the hand and floated across the stream and field of ripe corn, with scarecrows swaying in the wind, when they saw them flying overhead they waved to them.

Marcos thought this was hilarious. He was still holding Lacy's hand, and they flew over a river and landed in a lush green field. They landed with a gentle bump and Lacy threw her arms around him and she called him the jolly green giant and when he looked at his hands they were green.

He held on tight to Lacy he didn't want to let go of her, this was the women he wanted to live with till he grew old. He stroked her hair and caressed her face, she was Lacy, and she was the one. They lay on the ground wrapped in each other arms, Marcos fell fast asleep in her arms.

The doorbell rang and Marcos woke up, he again was in an armchair in his house. He stood up and stretched his arms and yawned loudly, and went to open the door.

It was his neighbour offering him some eggs from her hens. He was delighted and accepted them. He thought he would have scrambled eggs for tea. He went into the kitchen and put the kettle on, to make a cup of tea, and he wondered if he had been dreaming but he found grass on the back of his jumper. He had no logical answers to what is going on.

He had never dreamed such vivid dreams and never with the same woman in the dream. Maybe someone was trying to show him something or maybe his heart was yearning for his one true love. He thought he needed to start dating so he could find Lacy. He also knew that he needed to get those commissions done.

He rang his mum to tell her he was going to start looking for the love of his life, which surprised her as he had said he was going to be single until they put him in the ground. She told him there was a couple of nice ladies in her Zumba class. He tried to put her off but now the door was open for dinner parties and loads of ladies on a conveyer belt, and he wasn't sure if this was the way to find Lacy but you never know.

He started the painting of the church in Hoghton and he decided that he would do the second one later.

He sent some sketches to the couple for approval. He looked at the sketches and thought he would love to get married there and have their reception in Hoghton Tower, it was so much like a fairy tale and one day it could be his.

His mum phoned and said she was arranging a dinner party and she needed him to make up the numbers but he knew she was setting him up with a blind date. It was his own fault, he had given her the go ahead. He thought he may meet the one, maybe her name will not be Lacy, and so he needed to give his dinner partner a chance.

The day arrived, his mum had reminded him day before, she told him to dress smart and get the paint off his hands. He said he would, so he arrived about fifteen minutes before the meal. His mum checked him over, he felt like it was his first day at school. His mum approved and told him to go and answer the door. He recognised the first arrivals, they were his parents' long-time friends Jessie and Moses. They were surprised to see him, but they wanted to find out what he was up to.

The next arrivals were another couple Marcos did not know, Marcos's father introduced him to a new couple who had moved in next door and then arrived three people, a couple from his mum's yoga class and a lovely looking young lady whose name was Katie, she was full of smiles and seemed to know everyone in the room.

Doris introduced Marcos to Katie, and sat them next to each other at the table, Moses and Jessie sat at the table. Doris introduced Sandy and Michael to everyone, Wilf filled up everyone's glasses and then went to help Doris bring in the food. It was potato and leek soup, followed by roast beef and all the trimmings and then crumble and custard.

There was a problem as Katie was a vegetarian. Doris was very upset, as she didn't ask, Katie said it was fine, she would eat everything except the beef or gravy, and she would love a piece of fruit instead of crumble. Doris was so embarrassed by the oversight, Marcos tried to joke about vegetarians and vegans, and his mum gave him that look.

Everyone tried to lighten the atmosphere but it was already spoilt. Marcos tried to talk to Katie but she was very uptight and he found it hard to get a word out of her. The dinner seemed to go on and on. Crumble and custard were served and a banana was given to Katie. Doris offered them cheese and biscuits but they all declined and decided it was time to leave. Wilf and Doris gave them their coats and everyone thanked Doris for a wonderful meal.

Marcos helped to clear the dishes and pack the dishwasher. Doris was so upset that one of her guests had been embarrassed, Wilf tried to console her and turned the conversation to Marcos and Katie but Doris already knew she was not the one for him.

Marcos hadn't really enjoyed the dinner but at least he had dipped his toes in the water. He was desperate to find his one and only love.

He went to the suppliers to buy some canvases and oil paint, he had been going to the same place since he moved into the area, he had developed a good relationship with Joe who owned the suppliers.

They started to talk about what project Marcos was doing and his up-and-coming exhibition. They went to have coffee in the back of the shop. Joe introduced Marcos to his new girlfriend Maggie, he had met her online and he recommended Marcos to give it a try.

He showed Marcos the website he used and told him there was loads of websites on the internet. Joe offered to help him set up his profile and how to check out the women. Joe was really happy in his new relationship and wanted all his friends to be happy, so he was going to encourage them all to try internet dating. He also suggested lonely heart columns in newspapers, they might be old fashioned but his sister had found her husband that way and they had been married for ten years.

With all that encouragement Marcos would give it a go but only once he was done with his exhibition and had finished his latest commission. Joe made him promise.

Marcos went home and started on the commission and was working on the church in Hoghton. He had really fallen in love with the area, with the church, inside and out. He had a beautiful sketch and photo with the sun shining down through the trees, when he looked into the photo he noticed a figure of a person he didn't see before.

He needed to enlarge the photo and when he did he was shocked it was Lacy, he didn't remember seeing her that day. Maybe he needed to go back and see if she lived in the local village.

So the next day he went off Hoghton, he walked around the area showing people the photo of Lacy, but no one knew who she was. He went to speak to the vicar but she did not know her, he went to Hoghton Tower and spoke to the staff, who had never seen her. He thought he was going mad, he kept seeing her in his dreams and now in a photo.

He felt he needed to get on with his search for the love of his life, that person who he would love forever, just like his parents but he hoped it would be love at first sight on both sides. He already fallen love with Lacy but he thought he must not continue to look for Lacy, she was a person of his dreams.

Marcos went back to his house to get on with his canvases for his exhibition. He decided to use the lane up to the Tower as the starting point, he started out with a wash over of the canvas and using brushes and a palette knife, he had been really inspired to do a sleepy, dreamy scene with a horse and carriage driving up there. He had not drawn a horse for a long time but he was always good at animals. His tutor had always remarked how well he drew animals. He needed to get some photos or sketches of a carriage and horses. He checked the internet and found a perfect shot of horses and carriage, it would be ideal for his latest painting.

Once the wash was dry he began the painting. He felt inspired and spent hours on the painting, he didn't realise that it was dark outside and he had not stopped to eat. He stood back and checked his work, and was happy with the work he had done. It was too late to carry on so he went to make himself something to eat and drink.

Marcos decided he would start a profile and found it a puzzle, what to say about himself, how do you describe yourself? He felt out of his depth, so he decided tomorrow he would visit Joe again for some help.

He was just about to go off for an early night when his phone rang, it was his mum, she was inviting him for another dinner party, just his mum and dad and Lucy, and his mum thought she would ideal for him. She was a teacher and worked in the local high school where his dad worked as the caretaker. Marcos agreed to the dinner party, maybe she might be the one, but just in case he would go to Joe's.

Before he went to Joe's after he done a bit more work on the canvas of Hoghton Tower, he sat down on the stool facing the canvas, he could feel a cold breeze on the back of his head and suddenly felt water on this back, he turned right around and he was standing on the grass facing the Tower, it had begun to rain so he ran under a large tree and then he saw Lacy looking for him.

She shouted that she had given up. They had been playing hide and seek, he came out from the trees and called her name and she came running. She was soaking wet, so he took off his jacket and helped Lacy to put it on. They kissed and laughed and then decided to run up to the tower and get warm and have a warm drink.

They got to the tower and settled in front of the roaring fire and ordered tea and toast with jam, strawberry jam which they both loved. The tea and toast were put on a small table in front of the fire, they both were hungry and ate very quickly. Lacy got jam on her nose which Marcos kissed off.

They discussed their upcoming engagement party and the plan to get married in Hoghton church, he felt he couldn't be happier. He had the life he always craved, Lacy was funny, beautiful and clever, and she worked with children who had special needs. She was his ideal woman. She went off to the toilet and Marcos closed his eyes for a moment and he must have dropped off, when he opened his eyes he was in his sitting room.

He was devastated he had lost Lacy again. He went back into the art studio where he thought he had been sitting but he thought he must have gone into the sitting room but he didn't remember doing that, maybe he was a bit crazy, crazy with love, how would he ever find Lacy.

Well he needed to get online and find Lacy or maybe Lucy was Lacy, whatever it takes he would find her. He went to Joe's shop with his computer and they signed him up to hearts and flowers and completed all the information. He got a free trial for seven days, and he intended on using it well.

Marcos went home and started to swipe right, he looked at so many profiles but he couldn't find Lacy. He had to remind himself that Lacy was a dream girl, she wasn't real so he needed to give some of these women a chance. He thought he would go to dinner at his parents and meet Lucy and see how he got on. He would then ask his parents for their opinion of some of the women on the dating site.

Marcos arrived at his parents' home and was introduced to Lucy who had arrived early. She was beautiful, slim with long dark hair, not his usual type but neither is Lacy. They all enjoyed the meal and got on really well, he could see that his mum was happy it was going well. His dad was just happy that his wife was happy, no mishaps in the meal, Lucy ate everything that was offered.

After eating they all sat in the sitting room and chatted about the school and art, it all seemed to go so well. Doris had great hopes that this dinner would be the first of many, maybe she will see his boy married and hopefully there would be grandchildren.

When Lucy departed Marcos saw her out and they exchanged numbers. Once the front door was shut, Doris wanted to know how he felt, would he date her? Wilf told her to slow down and let Marcos speak.

Marcos told them she was wonderful and he would like to meet up with her again, how he could tell them that his heart had been stolen by a woman in his dreams. He needed to shake himself, here was a wonderful, sweet girl who could be good for him, he did like her and genuinely wanted to get to know her but he had to forget about Lacy but how?

Marcos phoned Lucy and suggested they meet up for drinks, she was delighted to meet up, she had just come out of a bad marriage, the divorce had been finalised and she was trying to build her life again. She had heard a lot about Marcos from his dad. This could be a good match, they had so much in common, and it could be a good start but let's wait and see. She had been so hurt so she was a bit cautious, but really wanted it to work.

Marcos was in the wine bar, feeling a bit uncomfortable as this was not his usual hangout, the wine bar had opened about a month ago. He hadn't ordered as he thought he would wait for Lucy. Lucy arrived looking beautiful, her hair was flowing, and she was wearing jeans and a cashmere jumper. He kissed her on the cheek and she sat down opposite him.

Marcos asked she wanted to drink, she asked for a white wine, he went over to the bar and ordered a white wine and a bottle of beer, he turned around to look at Lucy and could see other men admiring her, she gave him a big smile and he felt that he was the only one she was interested in. He went back to the table with the order, the conversation flowed and they stayed there for a few hours, laughing and chatting.

As it was their first date they decided not to go anywhere after the wine bar, so Marcos walked her to her car and kissed her on the cheek and promised to call her to arrange another date. He felt the date had gone well.

Just as he turned around he saw a red head walking away from him, he caught her face in the reflection in a shop window and it was Lacy. He ran after her as she turned the corner but by the time he got there she had disappeared. His heart was pounding, he told himself it was his imagination. He had met a wonderful woman Lucy, but his heart was with Lacy, how he could dislodge her from there.

He went home and picked up his paint brush to do some more work on the church in Hoghton, he stood back and liked what he saw. It had taken him a while to be happy with both canvases and needed to get them back to the couple who had commissioned them.

He thought it was too late to phone them now so he would do it the following morning, just as he was about to go to bed his phone rang. It was his mum, she wanted to know how the date went. He told her about the date but not about the sighting of Lacy, she would think he had gone mad.

He told her they were going to meet up soon but he had to finish off some more paintings for his exhibition, she told him not to keep her waiting as she could be snapped up by someone else, he promised he would phone her.

The next morning he phoned the couple to say the paintings were finished and he would frame them today and they could pick them up tomorrow or anytime they were able to. They said they were going away for a few days but would collect them as soon as possible after that. He was happy with that and hoped they will like them. This was always the time that an artist dreads, you may be happy with your work but you want the people who commissioned the work to be happy.

He went to phone Lucy but realised she would be in class with her students, so thought he would start a canvas, he took out the photos and sketches of the Trough of Bowland. He found one that he loved and began by putting a wash over the canvas. As it was an oil painting he needed to leave it to dry.

He went to sit at the kitchen table and check the dating site. He knew he had met someone who may be able to make him happy but what if Lacy was on this site? He swiped right but didn't find Lacy, there was a few matches which he looked at but felt he couldn't meet up with other women while he was getting to know Lucy.

Once the paint was dry he went back to start his painting of the Trough of Bowland, he put the outline in and then the phone rang it was Lucy, she asked how the couple liked the paintings. He told her they hadn't seen them yet, they were coming later in the week. He told her he was preparing for an exhibition so wouldn't have time to go on another date. Lucy suggested she could cook at home and bring it over, she would love to see his work and spend time with him.

Marcos was flattered and he arranged for her to come over in a couple of days. He thought this maybe be a really good idea and he would see Lucy in his home. He wished he could get Lacy out of his head and his heart.

He took out the painting of Hoghton Tower he had a few more tweaks to complete and then it would be a finished canvas for his exhibition. He sat back on his stool facing the canvas, he began to feel a warm breeze on his back, he thought he had left a window open and it was a warm breeze.

As he turned towards the window he was on the path going towards Hoghton Tower and he could see someone waving to him. It was Lacy, she looked so wonderful in a white flowing summer dress with a straw hat in her hand, and she was calling him to hurry up as the ice cream was melting in her hands. He started running towards her just as he got to her, there was a loud ringing and he turned around to see who was ringing and he was back in his living room and his front door bell was ringing. It was his dad Wilf, he had come over to see if there was anything he could help with for his exhibition, and his wife had sent him to find out if Marcos was going out with Lucy again.

Wilf loved to help and had framed some of Marcos's paintings before, so Marcos showed him the two commissions he had completed and were in need of framing. So Wilf took the paintings and went to get the tools and wood, he took them outside as it was a lovely day.

Marcos made them tea and went to the garden, they began talking, Wilf told him your mum asked me to come and find out what is happening with Lucy. He laughed because he knew that Marcos knew his mother would do this, so he told him that he and Lucy were fine, that she was coming over and she was bringing the food. Wilf thought his wife couldn't have predicted that. At least he could give her some good news.

Wilf arrived home, he hadn't got in the door and his wife wanted to know the news, he told her what Marcos had told him, but he said don't start planning a wedding, he sensed there was a bit of hesitation in Marcos but he didn't know why and Marcos didn't say anything.

Marcos got back to finishing the painting of Hoghton Tower. No more day dreaming, he got up to look at it from a far, he looked under the easel and there was a napkin with the tower's name on it. He thought he must have brought it back the last time he went, but when he picked it up it had a lipstick kiss on it. He didn't know how he could explain this, he couldn't.

He carried on with the painting depicting the Trough of Bowland, he always loved that area and would love to move there and buy a house with roses around the front door. He loved the winding lanes and the woods, it would be ideal to move when he got older, not so children friendly, you would become mum or dad taxi. He knew he needed to get ready for the exhibition or he wouldn't be able to pay his mortgage. He had so many ideas and had lots of photos and sketches.

As he was thinking about what to do next the phone rang and he went to answer it, it was an old friend Susan whom hadn't seen since university, she needed his help, she had found a lovely old painting but it needed some restoration and she knew he had done some restoration before., She needed it done as quickly as possible it was for her grandfather's 80th birthday, she begged him, he told her he was getting ready for an exhibition, she said she would help, she worked in computer graphics she could do his flyers and would help him to set up, so he agreed and she said she would be over in two hours.

Which she did and she arrived at the door bearing gifts of wine and pizza and the painting, Marcos took the painting and put it up on an easel. He was shocked, there was Lacy looking back at him, he turned around to Susan and asked her where she found it and who was the women in the picture. Susan said it was her grandfather's first love and he had lost her, he went to war and wasn't able to keep in contact as he was in a prisoner of war camp and when he did return she was gone, she had gone to be a nurse in Italy. He tried to find her but he couldn't he was broken hearted but his parents wanted him to be married and have an heir to take over the family business, so he had to give up but he never got over losing her. Then one day he saw this painting in a junk shop and he had to have it, and he got it, but it needs to be restored.

Marcos couldn't take it in, he started to check what needed to be done, it was very dull so it needed to be cleaned and it had a couple of tears which needed to be repaired, he told her that he would call her once he had done the restoration. She asked him if he would like to meet her grandfather, he was so overwhelmed, maybe he could find out the lady in the paintings name and how he married Susan's grandmother once he lost the love of his life, maybe he could help him get Lacy out of his heart so he could give it to Lucy.

It took him a few days to do the restoration, so he found he had put heart into the restoration, he wished he could keep it but it needed to be handed over to Susan's grandfather. He rang her and she gave him the address and said she would meet him there.

He drove over to Susan's grandfather's house, it wasn't his birthday today but she wanted him to have it as soon as he could. He drove up the street and arrived at the door and rang the bell, a well-dressed and sprightly old man, who greeted him with a shake of his hand.

Marcos followed him into his sitting room and Marcos explained that he had restored the painting and expected to meet Susan, he told him Susan was running late. So Marcos unwrapped the painting, Susan grandfather Joseph took one look and burst into tears, Marcos gave him a tissue and helped him to his seat, Joseph needed to look at the painting and asked Marcos to bring it closer, so Marcos pulled a chair nearer to him so he could see the painting better.

Marcos asked him her name he said Lacy, Marcos needed to sit down, he asked Joseph if he ever found her. He said he had she was in a care home. He had gone to look for a care home to move to as the house was too big for him and there she was, he asked the manager who showed him around her name, he said Lacy, she had never married, she had lost the love of her life and she had a good life but she never had any children. He told Marcos he didn't talk to her, he broke her heart, how could he just turn up, he had looked and looked but never found her.

Marcos asked him how he married someone else even though he loved Lacy. Joseph said he had to marry, it was expected of him. He met Susan's grandmother on a blind date, they got on, he knew she would never be the love of his life but she would be a good wife, and mother, which she was but she never filled his heart. Marcos said you need to go to the care home and spend the time with her. Joseph said he thought he could be right but at the moment he needed to look at the painting again and forever.

Susan arrived and was delighted with Marcos's work. She could see her grandfather was overwhelmed and still had tears in his eyes. It looked like Marcos had been crying as well. She asked her grandfather what he thought of the restoration, he hadn't spoken since she came in, he was focusing on the painting.

He said he loved the painting but it was bitter sweet, there was his first love and she was as beautiful as she had been when she waved him off as he took the train to go off to the war. Joseph had spent many days looking for her before he was told she was in Italy, as the war in Italy was still going on he wasn't allowed to go there to find her. He wanted to wait for her but his parents insisted he marry, he was the oldest son and his father was working to hand over the business to him.

Susan could not find the words to thank Marcos for the restoration. They left Joseph staring at the painting and went into the kitchen. Marcos asked if her grandmother was still alive, Susan said she had died ten years ago and her grandfather continued to live in the large house. He had considered moving into a care home, but after seeing Lacy he felt he couldn't move in there but it was the best in the area.

Marcos said she needs to persuade him to move there, why waste the rest of his life in a home he can't manage, when he could live with his first love. Susan said she would try and maybe Marcos could help her. They went back into the sitting room, Marcos said he would love to see Lacy as she is now. After much persuasion he agreed to go back with Susan and Marcos, so they phoned the care home and set off, as they pulled up in front of the care home Joseph began feel apprehensive, but Susan encouraged him and they went in.

Just as Lacy was going out, she looked up and saw Joseph, you could see the recognition in her eyes and she said Joseph is that you, she held out her hand, Joseph took it and kissed it, she asked him if he was moving in, he said yes, she said good we have so much to catch up on.

Susan and Marcos felt like gooseberries as Joseph and Lacy only had eyes for each other. So they left Lacy and Joseph sitting in the garden. Marcos looked at Lacy and she was an older version of his Lacy. Susan and Marcos went for a walk around the grounds, they came back about an hour later and they were still in deep conversation. Susan asked her grandfather if he was ready to go, he said he wanted to see the available flat in the care home, he didn't want to let Lacy go. They went into the home and spoke to the manager who was delighted that he wanted to move in and that he seemed to have a friend which would help him settle in.

So that was settled, Joseph would put his house up for sale and move in to the flat as soon as he can. Marcos asked Lacy if she had any family that might be concerned about her suddenly finding her first and only love, she said she didn't have any children of her own, but she had three nieces, one who was named Lacy and she explained people often think she was her daughter, Marcos's heart jumped in his chest, he asked her if she was in the area, Lacy said no, she had a high flying job which took her all over the world, she was engaged to a pilot but she was having cold feet, so they were having a break.

Marcos went home thinking this must be his Lacy, he needed to find her but how and what about Lucy, oh Lucy, how was he going to let her down, what if he never met Lacy. Was he willing to wait until he was going to retire to find her? He thought like Joseph's Lacy he would wait, no matter how long. Lucy was due that evening, he really liked her but he wasn't in love with her.

She arrived with a casserole and hot fresh bread. He greeted her with a kiss on the cheek, they went into the kitchen to put the casserole in the oven. They then went into Marcos's studio and she looked at some of his finished canvas and those he had started. She was really interested in his paintings and loved the Hoghton Tower, she asked him if he would take her there. He changed the conversation and said they needed to check the oven,

Lucy noticed but didn't say anything. They took out the food and put it on the table, it smelt wonderful, it was Lancashire hotpot. Lucy served him and they ripped the bread apart and dunked it in the hotpot.

After food Marcos washed up while Lucy sat at the table, she turned the conversation around to dating and how their track records matched up but Marcos was a little nervous as he hadn't really done much serious dating, he had only just started dating and she was his first and he really liked her but his heart was already stolen by Lacy. Lucy had seen that Marcos had pulled back since their last date and she wanted to know if there was any future for them., She didn't want to mess around with her heart, she had had a bad marriage and wasn't willing to waste her time. She wanted love but no messing around. So she decided she would be courageous, she took a deep breath and asked Marcos if he saw them develop a relationship, he was surprised but in a way it would be better to be honest.

So he told her he liked her but his heart had been given to another, she asked by whom, he was reluctant to tell her, he thought she would think he is mad. He told her about his dreams but also finding grass on this back and other things, such as sitting on a stool and he wakes up in his sitting room. She thought that was amazing and he should and try and find Lacy. Marcos thanked her for her understanding and said if she ever needed a plus one, he would be there for her. She said she will do that. She collected the casserole dish and thanked him for a wonderful evening.

News got back to his parents that he was no longer dating Lucy and they wanted to know why, so instead of phoning them he drove to their house. He saw them through the window and knew he was in for interrogation, he opened the door, his hands were full of paint, he was trying out using acrylics with his hands, when his mum saw it, it took her back to Marcos's childhood when they did handprint painting.

She went straight into the kitchen to make coffee for them, she had brought some biscuits with them. Then they went to sit in his garden, Doris thought she needed to come over and tidy up the garden. Once they sat down Wilf said he had met Lucy in the school and he asked her how dinner went, she told him it went well but they are not taking their relationship to anything other than friendship, but she wasn't heart broken, so his parents wanted to know if he was heartbroken but they could see he wasn't, but they wanted to know what happened.

Marcos tried to explain to his parents about Lacy, his mum couldn't get her mind around what he is telling them, how can be in love with a woman in his dreams and lose Lucy, she thought he had lost his mind. Wilf tried to calm her down and to see that is Lucy wasn't the one its better they don't get to attached.

He told her Lucy was fine with it, so she should not be too hard on their son, when the right person comes along he will forget about Lacy. She still was not happy but could see that Lucy has moved on.

So they drank coffee and then Marcos showed them some of the canvases he had completed, they were so happy to see what he had done, they loved the Hoghton tower and ask him where it was, he told them not far from Preston. Doris told Wilf that they should go and see it themselves. Doris seem to have put her disappointment behind and hoped he would find the love of his life, as long as he is not waiting around for the woman of his dreams or at least not Lacy.

Marcos wanted to find out more about Joseph and his Lacy, maybe she could tell him more about his Lacy and where she was and how he could meet her, he know she was engaged but he needed to change her mind. He phoned Susan and ask if her grandfather had moved to the care home and she said he was due to move and was packing and sorting out his years of belongings, if he had time on his hands he would be of help, tomorrow would be ideal. So he agreed to go to Joseph's home to help in any way he could.

But now he had to complete more canvases, he had finished the one of Hoghton Tower, he thought he might keep that for himself. He finished the acrylic painting using his hands, he sat on the stool facing the painting and with his back to the mirror, and the painting was very abstracted, he stared at it and as he did, he found himself sitting in a big top, and there where clowns and jugglers, and a ballerina on the back of a horse, he watched with amazement, she was standing on a bare back horse, she had a harness on so she wouldn't fall, she saw him and gave him little wave and smile. It was Lacy, he sat still and wiped his eyes, how can she be here, he thought he must be dreaming and anything can happen in a dream.

At the end of the act the crowd clapped really loud and the horse and Lacy left the ring. The ring master came to where he was sitting and told him Lacy was waiting for him in her caravan. He nodded and set off to find Lacy's caravan, he knew which one to go to but he had never been there before. She opened the door and jumped into Marcos arms and kissed him. He kissed her back and they went inside the caravan, he looked around it was like a pink palace, it made him laugh, she asked him why he was laughing, he told her because she made him so happy.

She got changed and ready to go out for the evening, she had done her last ride for the night and she wanted to go and eat out, so Marcos took her hand and they ran towards the town, but he had no idea where he was, but he saw a restaurant and suggested they went there.

She told him to order for her while she went to the ladies, how was supposed to order he had no idea, he picked up the menu and thankfully no waiter or waitress came to him before she came back, she looked at the menu and he asked what if we try something new to eat, which she thought was a fun idea and she said lets have all vegetarian meals tonight, he said fine, he know this had got him out of a hole.

So she chose really odd meals but they enjoyed trying them, but most of all they enjoyed each other company. Marcos could not take his eyes off her, he made her blush. There was music playing and he had asked her to dance, so they did a very slow dance, enjoying each other's body and kissing until the music stopped. They paid up and went back to the circus and Lacy caravan. She told him they were moving on tomorrow and thank him for a wonderful week, but he begged her to stay, that she wasn't just a week holiday romance, he loved her and wanted to marry her, she laughed at him and pushed him out of the caravan and locked the door.

Marcos was not going home, he would follow her wherever she went, he found an old sack and lay on the floor on top of the sack waiting for the morning, and he closed his eyes and slept off.

He woke up asleep in his sitting room, he had been lying on a sack on his floor, now he thought this was getting weird, he went into the studio and checked the area, he saw the stool he sat on and the window and the mirror, all these happenings had been happening since he found the mirror, what magic did this mirror have. He decided he was losing his mind, it cannot be a mirror it must be him, he must have fallen asleep on the floor in his sitting room, but where did he get the sack and the other things from. The only thing he knew was that he wanted to find Lacy. He needed to find her.

He went over to help Joseph pack up. Joseph was so happy to see him. He began to tell him again about Lacy and how much he loved her, he couldn't wait to move into the care home, his flat was only two doors down from his, he even told him he was going to propose to Lacy before it was too late. Marcos felt he could talk to him about his Lacy. So they sat down with a cup of tea and Marcos explained to him his desire to find his own Lacy and that he had had dreams about her and when he restored the painting he saw Lacy there, not Joseph's Lacy but his and he needed to find her.

Joseph understood and said how he could help him. Marcos was not sure, but he wanted to talk to Joseph's Lacy, maybe she might have some photos of her niece Lacy maybe she would not be his Lacy but she might be, so Joseph said that he was going over to the care home tomorrow at noon to have lunch with Lacy and then move in, Susan was supervising the removal men. So they agreed to meet at the care home.

Marcos went home and did some more paintings, he decided to move the mirror over to the other side of the room, just in case but what if he would miss out seeing Lacy. It seemed such a mad idea that a mirror could do magic. Nothing happened that night and he went to bed with ideas of what he would find out from Joseph's Lacy.

Marcos went over to the care home by noon. Joseph and Lacy where already in the dining area, they had a third chair at their table for him. He sat down and Lacy asked him to tell her about his Lacy, he felt a bit stupid but told them both the dreams and about the painting the Joseph had found.

She told him her niece was an artist and had had many showings around the world, the last one was in Barbados, like his first dream, but she was travelling at the moment, she had become engaged but she called it off. She said she had met her love of her life and was waiting to see him again. Marcos was worried what if she had meet someone else. Lacy got out some photos, her niece Lacy had the same red hair, though Joseph Lacy hair had gone white with age, her niece looked like Lacy in the painting her had restored and he knew she was the one.

Joseph Lacy didn't know where she was in the world now, but would try and find out, she didn't want anyone to be separated from their one and only love. She had to wait so long for Joseph and would never let him go. So she would speak to her sister to find out for him and she would let Joseph know. Marcos stayed for lunch and then went to help Susan unpack.

He did not hear from Joseph for a few weeks, and he was ready to give up, and he had had no more dreams, he even put the mirror back into its position but no dreams, he so wanted to hold Lacy in his arms and to kiss her.

He knew he had to get on with the exhibition and his mum was still trying to find him the one, his friend Joe was telling him to go online. He just told them both he was completing his painting for this exhibition and would try again after that, that satisfied Joe but not his mum, but she would keep looking.

The exhibition was all set up, Marcos had hired a catering company to hand out finger food and wine or orange juice. He was not sure how many would come, Joe was coming, also Susan who brought Joseph and Lacy with her, his parents were first as they always were. Susan had done the publicity for his exhibition and there had been a lot of interest in it.

It started out very slow but a couple of hours later there was a number of people looking at his work, one couple wanted to buy the Hoghton Tower but he could not let it go. He sold a number of paintings and the local newspaper had taken photos for their paper and online, so hopefully he will sell more. Lucy came with Stephen, she had met him at work, he was a teacher, and he was surprised his parents had not told him. Marcos was happy for her and Stephen, they seemed so in love. That is just why he wanted to meet his Lacy.

Just as the door was being locked for that night, another day tomorrow, there was a knock at the door, one of the waiters answered the door and said they were closed, but the person said she had to see Marcos, he opened the door and there walked in was Lacy. Her aunty Lacy had sent her a photo of Marcos and she knew he was the one in her dreams. He was the love of her life, she had been in South Africa and had to get the next flight over so she wouldn't lose him again.

Marcos was taken back, standing in front of him was his Lacy, she throw her arms around his neck and they kissed. His parents, friends and Joseph and Lacy stood watching. They had not believed there was a Lacy, that he was going mad, but she was standing there, Marcos introduced her to his family and friends. There was no introduction needed to her aunty but to Joseph she felt she had known him all her life, she knew everything about her aunt's love of her life and could see the love between Joseph and Lacy.

She was so happy to be with Marcos and he was frightened that it was a dream and she would disappear, so he held onto her hand and they closed the door to the exhibition and Marcos and Lacy went home. He showed her around what would be their home and he went into the studio to show her the mirror which had caused him to dream, but it was gone, they looked everywhere but it was gone. He thought the mirror's work was done. He was the happiest he had ever been and ever will be. He decided he was never going to lose Lacy again, so he went on one knee and asked her to marry him, he didn't have a ring but he had made one with a piece of wire and they could go and buy another tomorrow and start planning their marriage and their life together.